Love to Miranda
From
Gramma and
Granpa Don
(Christmas 1998)

Published by
Grandreams Limited
Jadwin House, 205/211 Kentish Town Road, London,
NW5 2JU.

Printed in Italy.

BW9-12

THE TIN SOLDIER

Illustrated by Pam Storey.
Stories re-told by Grace De La Touche.

1

Once upon a time, there were twenty five little tin soldiers. They were identical brothers as they had all been made from the same tin spoon. They all shouldered their rifles and stood looking forward. Their uniforms were of red and blue and they looked really splendid when they stood in a long line.

They lived in the

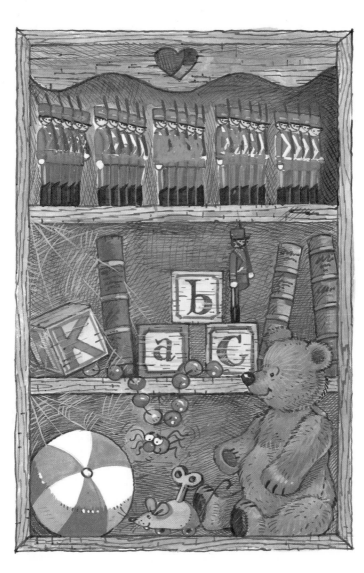

nursery on the third floor, and the first words they ever heard were those cried out by the little boy who owned them. "Tin soldiers!" he cried, when he opened the box on his birthday.

The little boy took them out and stood them up in a row. They were all identical in every way, except for the last tin soldier. Sadly, when he was being made, there

hadn't been enough tin to finish him off, and he therefore stood on just one leg. But he was a steadfast tin soldier, and stood just as firmly on his one leg as his brothers did on their two legs. This made him stand out. He was as beautifully painted as his brothers, and was proud to be one of the tin soldiers.

The little boy was given many other toys on

his birthday, and these were on the table with the tin soldier. One which caught the tin soldier's eye was a splendid paper castle. You could see through the tiny windows right into the castle rooms. He looked and looked, imagining himself as a soldier on guard at the castle. At the front of the castle was a tiny lake surrounded by trees. It was really a mirror, but it looked like water as some tiny wax swans were swimming around on it, reflected in the surface.

It was all very pretty, but the prettiest part of all was the little dancing lady who stood at the castle door. She also was made of paper, but she wore a skirt of bright muslin, with a narrow blue ribbon around her waist and over her

shoulder. Glued to the ribbon was a twinkling spangle.

The little lady stretched her arms high above her head, for she was a dancer. She had one leg raised so high in the air, that the soldier could not work out where it was, and was sure that she must be one-legged like himself.

"She would be the

perfect wife for me!" thought the little tin soldier. "But she's such a fine lady. She lives in a beautiful castle and I live in a dark wooden box with all my brothers! That's no place for her. Still, I shall have to do what I can to get to know her."

At that moment he was lying behind a snuff box on the table away from his brothers, and he

had an excellent view of
the castle and of the pretty
little lady who could stand
so long on one leg without
falling over.

Later that evening,
when the family went to
bed, the little boy put the
tin soldiers back in their
box - that was all except
the little tin soldier with one
leg, who was still behind

the snuff box.

As soon as the house was quiet, the toys began to play. They played the games that they wanted to play, visiting the toys they hadn't seen all day, meeting and making friends with the new toys.

The tin soldiers jumped up and down in their box, rattling the lid,

trying to get out and join in the fun, but they couldn't get the lid off.

All the toys made so much noise that they woke up the canary. The canary, not to be outdone, joined in, chirping away to the noise.

The only two who said nothing and who made no move were the one-legged tin soldier and the little dancer outside

her castle. She still stood on tiptoe, her arms stretched high above her head, and he stood on his one leg, never taking his bright painted eyes off her.

Suddenly, as the clock in the nursery struck midnight, the lid of the snuff box beside the little tin soldier flew open! But there was no snuff in it, instead there was a little goblin, a tricky little jack-in-the-box.

"I know you tin soldier," said the jack-in-the-box slyly. "Just you keep your eyes to yourself!"

But the little tin soldier pretended to ignore him and continued to gaze at the dancer.

"Very well," said the jack-in-the-box, "just you wait until morning!"

❸

Morning came, and the children got up and came straight to the nursery to play with the toys, new and old. The little tin soldier was found, and put up on the window sill.

Now, whether it was a draught, or the wishes of the naughty jack-in-the-box, suddenly the nursery window sprang open and the poor little toy soldier tumbled out. He fell head

first from the third floor nursery window. The fall was over extremely quickly and the little tin soldier found himself landing upside down on his helmet, with the bayonet on his rifle sticking in between two paving slabs.

The nursery maid and the little boy ran straight down the stairs and out onto the street looking for

the little tin soldier. They very nearly trod on him, but they didn't see him.

Now maybe if he had cried out, "Here I am!" they would have found him. But he didn't think it the right thing to do to call out when he had his uniform on.

It suddenly started to rain, and the maid took the little boy back into the house giving up the search.

"Never mind little master," said the maid. "We'll have another look when the rain stops. Let's go and play with the other toys."

The rain came down faster and faster, until it was a heavy downpour. The little tin soldier couldn't move.

Eventually it stopped, and along the street came two young urchins. "Look at this!" cried one of them, bending over to pick up the toy. "It's a little tin soldier!"

"Let's build him a boat!" said the other. "Let's send him sailing off!"

They made a boat from newspaper, and then placing the little tin soldier inside, they put the boat in the water running in the gutter. They ran alongside, clapping their hands as

the little boat floated down
the fast current. The recent
rain filled the gutter, and
the little boat bobbed up
and down, and now and
again it would spin right
round in the current. This
made the little tin soldier
feel very giddy, but he did
not complain. He
remained the steadfast
little tin soldier, never
flinching, his eyes forward
and his rifle held against

his shoulder.

The rain swept the little boat along, but suddenly it went dark as the water whirled down into a covered drain.

"Oh, no!" cried the boys, as they watched the boat disappear from sight. "We've lost it!"

It was as dark as the little tin soldier's wooden box where he lived with his twenty four brothers.

"What is going to happen to me now?" asked the little tin soldier. "It's all that jack-in-the-box's fault! If only the little dancing lady were with me in this little boat! It wouldn't seem half as dark then."

"Passport!" a voice

suddenly cried out. It was a water rat who lived down the drain. "Have you got a passport? Where is your passport?" it demanded.

But the little tin soldier said nothing. He held onto his rifle, and staring straight ahead, the little tin soldier in the boat sailed past the angry water rat.

"Stop!" cried the rat, gnashing its teeth and chasing after the boat.

"Stop that boat. He hasn't paid the toll! I haven't seen his passport! He doesn't have a passport! Stop him!"

The current grew faster and faster, and the soldier could suddenly see daylight ahead of him. The drain was coming to an end, and the water poured out. The little tin soldier could hear the water roaring and rushing out of

the hole. It poured out into a great canal. For the little tin soldier, it was as dangerous as us sailing off a giant waterfall!

The boat was rushing along so fast, the tin soldier couldn't stop if he had tried, and a moment later the little newspaper boat flew out of the hole and was thrown out into the rushing water of a canal.

The little boat twirled

and span, slowly sinking.
The poor little tin soldier
held himself as stiffly as he
could, no-one could say
that he flinched. The boat
was sent spinning once,
twice, three times and the
water rose in the boat.
Deeper and deeper rose
the water until it was up to
the little tin soldier's neck.
And then the newspaper
boat started to break up,
and the water went over

the little tin soldier's head.

Suddenly the boat disappeared beneath the water, taking the brave little tin soldier with it. His last thoughts were of the pretty little lady standing outside her castle.

'Now I shall never get to know her,' he thought sadly.

❺

The paper boat broke up and the little tin soldier sank. But he was in for an even greater shock!

A huge great fish swam up and swallowed the little tin soldier!

"What now?" he asked as he lay in the fish's stomach. "My, it's so dark in here! Even darker than the drain!"

The little tin soldier

couldn't move much, so he remained lying steadfast, his rifle against his shoulder, and his eyes staring straight ahead.

The fish swam about, but then it began to dance about, twisting and turning horribly.

'What is happening?' wondered the little tin soldier.

The fish was suddenly

still. And then there seemed to be a flash of lightning passing through it! The light continued to shine, and then the little tin soldier heard a voice call out, "A tin soldier!"

The fish had been caught in the canal, taken to market and sold. It was then taken to a house and put on a table in the kitchen. The cook had

taken a sharp knife to cut it open, and much to her surprise had cut open the fish to find the little tin soldier.

The cook picked up the little soldier, and gave him to a maid. She gave him a quick wash, and then took him off through the house. All the time he stared straight ahead, rifle against his shoulder.

⑥

The little tin soldier was taken into a room, a nursery. He was stood on a table, and the maid told the family where he had been found, about the marvellous journey he had been on!

The little tin soldier stood on his one leg on the

table and looked around, and imagine his joy when he saw familiar children, and familiar toys standing on the table. He saw his family of tin soldiers standing by their box. Then he saw the pretty paper castle - and there still standing outside on one leg was the little dancer! It was a strange world! For he was back in the nursery!

If the little tin soldier could have cried, he would have done so. He was so touched. But that wouldn't have done at all. He looked at the pretty little dancer and she looked back at him.

Suddenly, one of the little boys, without ever saying why, grabbed hold of the

little tin soldier and hurled him into the fire! This was definitely the work of the jack-in-the-box.

The little tin soldier began to glow, and was feeling uncomfortably hot - but it was hard to say whether it was purely from the heat of the fire or from love of the little dancer. He was losing his lovely blue and red uniform, but

whether he had lost it on his travels or from the fire no-one could say. He could still see the little lady, and he continued to stare at her, his bright eyes looking forward. And the steadfast little soldier that he was, he still shouldered his rifle as he felt himself melting away.

Suddenly the nursery door opened, and a gust

of wind blew in. It caught hold of the little dancing lady outside her castle and she flew into the fire to land beside the little tin soldier. As she was made of paper, she burst into flames and was gone! The little tin soldier melted away to a lump of tin.

The following day, when the maid cleared out the hearth, she found what was left of the little tin soldier in a heart-shaped lump of tin. There was nothing left of the little dancing lady, except the spangle, and that was as black as soot and ruined.